CLASSICS Illustrated®

Charlotte Brontë
JANE EYRE

essay by
David Hoover, Ph.D.
New York University

ACCLAIM BOOKS
STUDY GUIDE

Jane Eyre

by Charlotte Bronte

JANE EYRE IS TEN YEARS OLD AS THE STORY OPENS. AN ORPHAN ALMOST FROM BIRTH, SHE IS HATED AND SHUNNED BY HER AUNT, MRS. REED, AND HER THREE COUSINS, JOHN, GEORGIANA AND ELIZA, OWNERS OF GATESHEAD HALL WHERE JANE LIVES. HER ONLY SOLACE IS AN OCCASIONAL KINDNESS SHOWN HER BY THE NURSE, BESSIE. ON A COLD, WINTER'S DAY, MRS. REED AND HER CHILDREN ARE GROUPED AROUND THE FIRE IN THE DRAWING ROOM...

JOHN REED

MRS. REED

JANE EYRE

BROCKLEHURST

ROCHESTER

MISS TEMPLE

Illustrated by
Harley M. Griffiths

SEATING HIMSELF IN AN ARM-CHAIR, HE MOTIONED HER TO STAND BEFORE HIM...

I CAN'T TAKE ANOTHER BEATING FROM HIM! I JUST CAN'T!

WITHOUT SPEAKING, HE STRUCK SUDDENLY AND STRONGLY...

THAT IS FOR YOUR IMPUDENCE IN ANSWERING MAMA A WHILE SINCE, AND FOR THE LOOK YOU HAD IN YOUR EYES, RAT! WHAT WERE YOU DOING BEHIND THE CURTAIN?

I WAS READING!

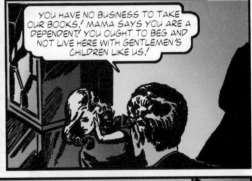

YOU HAVE NO BUSINESS TO TAKE OUR BOOKS! MAMA SAYS YOU ARE A DEPENDENT! YOU OUGHT TO BEG AND NOT LIVE HERE WITH GENTLEMEN'S CHILDREN LIKE US!

PICKING UP A HEAVY BOOK, HE HURLED IT AT HER...

GO AND STAND BY THE DOOR, OUT OF THE WAY OF THE MIRRORS AND WINDOWS!

SHE THRUST JANE BACK INTO THE ROOM AND LOCKED HER IN...

I MUST TEACH THE LITTLE IMP TO CONTROL HER VIOLENT TEMPER!

AS SHE HEARD THE KEY TURN IN THE LOCK EVERYTHING WENT BLACK...

NEXT THING JANE REMEMBERED WAS WAKING UP AS THOUGH FROM A NIGHTMARE. SHE HEARD VOICES SPEAKING WITH A HOLLOW SOUND AND FELT HERSELF BEING LIFTED UP AND PLACED IN A SITTING POSITION. GRADUALLY HER MIND CLEARED...

SHE RECOGNIZED MR. LLOYD, AN APOTHECARY, SOMETIMES CALLED IN BY MRS. REED WHEN THE SERVANTS WERE AILING...

WELL, MY CHILD, DO YOU KNOW WHO I AM?

YES, YOU ARE MR. LLOYD. HOW DO YOU DO, SIR?

WE SHALL DO VERY WELL BY AND BY, MY CHILD. I'LL RETURN TOMORROW.

BESSIE, WHAT IS THE MATTER WITH ME? AM I ILL?

YOU FELL SICK IN THE RED ROOM - WITH CRYING, I SUPPOSE! YOU'LL BE BETTER SOON, NO DOUBT! CALL IF YOU NEED ME!

FINALLY...

TELL ME, MISS JANE, WOULD YOU LIKE TO GO TO SCHOOL?

I SHOULD INDEED LIKE TO GO TO SCHOOL.

WELL, WELL, WHO KNOWS WHAT WILL HAPPEN?

THE CHILD OUGHT TO HAVE A CHANGE OF AIR AND SCENE,' NERVES NOT IN A GOOD STATE,'

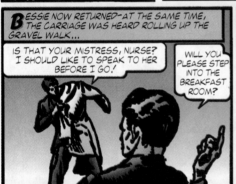

BESSIE NOW RETURNED–AT THE SAME TIME, THE CARRIAGE WAS HEARD ROLLING UP THE GRAVEL WALK...

IS THAT YOUR MISTRESS, NURSE? I SHOULD LIKE TO SPEAK TO HER BEFORE I GO!

WILL YOU PLEASE STEP INTO THE BREAKFAST ROOM?

SEVERAL WEEKS LATER...

AH, THERE YOU ARE, BRAT! I'VE GOT A FEW THINGS TO SETTLE WITH YOU!

FROM HER TALK WITH MR. LLOYD, AND FROM SCRAPS OF CONVERSATION SHE OVERHEARD BETWEEN THE SERVANTS, JANE SENSED A CHANGE IN HER EXISTENCE AND SHE GATHERED NEW COURAGE...

THIS TIME, JANE LASHED OUT AT HER TORMENTER WITH ALL HER PENT-UP FURY...

CHRISTMAS PASSED WITH THE USUAL FESTIVITIES AT GATESHEAD. JANE HOWEVER, WAS SHUNNED AND EXCLUDED FROM EVERY ENJOYMENT. ONE JANUARY MORNING, SHE WAS SEATED IN THE WINDOW-SEAT WHEN A CARRIAGE ROLLED UP THROUGH THE GATES...

I WONDER WHO THAT CAN BE? AS USUAL, I SUPPOSE ITS NO ONE INTERESTED IN ME!

SOON, BESSIE CAME RUNNING INTO THE NURSERY...

MISS JANE, TAKE OFF YOUR PINAFORE! HAVE YOU WASHED YOUR HANDS AND FACE THIS MORNING?

NO, BESSIE, I HAVE ONLY JUST FINISHED DUSTING!

TROUBLESOME, CARELESS CHILD! COME ALONG WITH ME!

BESSIE HAULED HER TO THE WASH-STAND AND INFLICTED A MERCILESS SCRUB ON HER HANDS AND FACE...

NOW, GO DIRECTLY DOWN TO THE BREAKFAST ROOM— AND MIND YOU, BE ON YOUR BEST MANNERS!

IN A FEW DAYS A COACH ARRIVED AND JANE TOOK LEAVE OF BESSIE...

GOOD-BYE, BESSIE!

OH, MISS JANE...

SHE WAS LITERALLY TAKEN FROM BESSIE'S NECK, TO WHICH SHE CLUNG WITH KISSES...

COME ON, MISS, WE CAN'T HOLD THE COACH!

AY, AY!

BE SURE AND TAKE CARE OF HER!

YES!

IS THERE A LITTLE GIRL CALLED JANE EYRE HERE?

A TEACHER FETCHED JANE FROM THE COACH.

FAR INTO THE AFTERNOON THE COACH ROLLED ON THROUGH MANY TOWNS AND OPEN COUNTRY. AT DUSK IT DREW UP BEFORE A WALL, BEYOND WHICH LOOMED A GROUP OF HOUSES...

INSTITUTION? JUST WHAT DOES THAT MEAN? AND JUST WHAT IS THE CONNECTION BETWEEN THE FIRST WORDS AND THE VERSE OF SCRIPTURES?

LOWOOD INSTITUTION
This portion was rebuilt by Naomi Brocklehurst of Bocklehurst Hall in this County. *Let your light shine before men that they may see your good works and glorify your Father which is in heaven.*

HER REVERIES WERE INTERRUPTED BY A SLIGHT COUGH BEHIND HER...

CAN YOU TELL ME WHAT THAT WRITING OVER THE DOOR MEANS? WHAT IS LOWOOD INSTITUTION?

WHY, THIS PLACE, OF COURSE! IT IS PARTLY A CHARITY SCHOOL — YOU AND I AND ALL THE REST ARE CHARITY CHILDREN!

WHO WAS NAOMI BROCKLEHURST?

THE LADY WHO BUILT THE NEW PART OF THIS HOUSE AND WHOSE SON OVERLOOKS AND DIRECTS EVERYTHING HERE!

THEN THIS PLACE DOES NOT BELONG TO MISS TEMPLE?

OH, NO! I WISH IT DID! SHE HAS TO ANSWER TO MR. BROCKLEHURST FOR ALL SHE DOES! MR. BROCKLEHURST BUYS ALL OUR FOOD AND ALL OUR CLOTHES.

MORE QUESTIONS FOLLOWED, INTERRUPTED BY THE SUMMONS FOR DINNER, THEN CAME MORE CLASSES. ANOTHER MEAL CONSISTING OF A SMALL MUG OF COFFEE AND A HALF SLICE OF BROWN BREAD, AND BEDTIME. SUCH WAS JANE EYRE'S FIRST DAY AT LOWOOD...

THE FOLLOWING DAY...

YOU DIRTY, DISAGREEABLE GIRL! YOU HAVE NEVER CLEANED YOUR NAILS THIS MORNING!

WHY DOES SHE NOT EXPLAIN THAT SHE COULD NEITHER CLEAN HER NAILS NOR WASH HER FACE, AS THE WATER WAS FROZEN!

THE TEACHER, MISS SCATCHERD, INFLICTED A DOZEN STROKES ON THE GIRL'S BACK...

HARDENED GIRL! NOTHING CAN CORRECT YOU OF YOUR SLATTERNLY HABITS - CARRY THE ROD AWAY!

JANE SAW THE TRACE OF A TEAR GLISTENING ON HER CHEEK AS SHE EMERGED FROM THE BOOK CLOSET...

I AM SLATTERNLY IN MY HABITS! WHEN I SHOULD BE LISTENING TO MISS SCATCHERD, MY MIND CONTINUALLY ROVES - I FALL INTO A SORT OF DREAM! SOMETIMES, I THINK THE NOISES I HEAR AROUND ME ARE THE BUBBLING OF A LITTLE BROOK NEAR OUR HOME, AND WHEN IT BECOMES MY TURN TO REPLY, I HAVE TO BE AWAKENED!

SHE WAS INTERRUPTED BY ONE OF THE MONITORS...

HELEN BURNS, IF YOU DON'T GO AND PUT YOUR DRAWER IN ORDER AND FOLD UP YOUR WORK THIS MINUTE, I'LL TELL MISS SCATCHERD!

WITH A SIGH, HELEN GOT UP AND LEFT...

WHAT A PITY! SHE IS SO SWEET AND CLEVER BUT ENTIRELY LACKING IN SPIRIT, I'M AFRAID!

THREE WEEKS LATER, JANE WAS PUZZLING OVER A SUM IN LONG DIVISION, WHEN SUDDENLY...

MR. BROCKLEHURST! I'VE BEEN LOOKING FORWARD WITH DREAD TO THE DAY OF HIS ARRIVAL, AND NOW HE IS HERE!

A FEW MOMENTS LATER...

THE LAUNDRESS TELLS ME SOME OF THE GIRLS HAVE TWO TUCKERS IN THE WEEK.' IT IS TOO MUCH — THE RULES LIMIT THEM TO ONE.'

I THINK I CAN EXPLAIN THAT, SIR.' TWO OF THE GIRLS HAD TEA WITH SOME FRENDS AT LOWTON AND I ALLOWED THEM THE EXTRA TUCKERS FOR THE OCCASION.'

WELL, DO NOT LET IT OCCUR TOO OFTEN.' ANOTHER THING — I FIND THAT A LUNCH COSISTING OF BREAD AND CHEESE HAS TWICE BEEN SERVED TO THE GIRLS.' WHO INTRODUCED THIS INNOVATION, AND BY WHAT AUTHORITY?

I DID, SIR.' THE BREAKFAST WAS ILL-PREPARED AND I DARED NOT ALLOW THEM TO GO HUNGRY 'TIL DINNER TIME.'

MADAME, WE MUST NOT ACCUSTOM THESE GIRLS TO LUXURY AND INDULGENCE.' BY OVERFEEDING THEIR BODIES, YOU LITTLE THINK HOW YOU MIGHT STARVE THEIR IMMORTAL SOULS.'

AS HE SPOKE, JANE'S SLATE SLIPPED FROM HER GRASP...

OH.'

IT IS THE NEW PUPIL, I PERCEIVE.' I MUST NOT FORGET I HAVE A WORD TO SAY RESPECTING HER.'

LET THE CHILD WHO BROKE HER SLATE COME FORWARD.'

DON'T BE AFRAID, JANE! I SAW IT WAS AN ACCIDENT - YOU SHALL NOT BE PUNISHED!

ORDERING JANE TO BE PLACED ON A STOOL, HE ADDRESSED THE CLASS...

MISS TEMPLE, TEACHERS AND CHILDREN YOU ALL SEE THIS GIRL! WHO WOULD THINK THAT THE EVIL ONE HAD ALREADY FOUND A SERVANT AND AGENT IN ONE SO YOUNG! YET, SUCH, I GRIEVE TO SAY, IS THE CASE!

YOU MUST BE ON YOUR GUARD AGAINST HER; IF NECESSARY AVOID HER COMPANY AND EXCLUDE HER FROM YOUR SPORTS! THIS CHILD IS A LIAR!

HE PROCEEDED TO LEAVE THE ROOM, THEN TURNED TOWARD MISS TEMPLE...

LET HER STAY HALF AN HOUR LONGER ON THAT STOOL AND LET NO ONE SPEAK TO HER DURING THE REMAINDER OF THE DAY!

I CAN'T STAND THE SHAME OF IT ALL! HE CALLED ME A LIAR BEFORE ALL THOSE PEOPLE! I WISH I WERE DEAD!

A WEEK LATER...

I HAVE INQUIRED INTO THE CHARGES MADE AGAINST MISS EYRE, AND I AM HAPPY TO SAY SHE IS INNOCENT!

MONTHS PASSED, AND IN THE SPRING, THE TERRIBLE SCOURGE OF TYPHUS SWEPT THE SCHOOL. SOME DIED AND WERE BURIED QUICKLY AND QUIETLY.

THERE'S DR. BATES, I THINK HE'S CALLING ON HELEN BURNS! THEY SAY SHE IS VERY ILL.

ONE NIGHT...

HELEN! GOOD HEAVENS — I MUST GET TO SEE HER SOMEHOW!

LEARNING THAT HELEN WAS IN MISS TEMPLE'S ROOM, JANE STOLE UP THE SIDE ENTRANCE, OPENED HER DOOR...

HELEN! ARE YOU AWAKE?

CAN IT BE YOU, JANE?

WHY HAVE YOU COME, JANE? IT IS PAST ELEVEN O'CLOCK — I HEARD IT STRIKE SOME MINUTES SINCE!

I CAME TO SEE YOU, HELEN — I HEARD YOU WERE VERY ILL AND I COULD NOT SLEEP TILL I HAD SPOKEN TO YOU!

HELEN PUT HER ARM AROUND JANE AND NESTLED CLOSE TO HER. AFTER A LONG SILENCE, SHE RESUMED, STILL WHISPERING...

EIGHT YEARS PASSED, AND JANE EYRE, NOW A YOUNG LADY OF EIGHTEEN, TAKES A POSITION AS GOVERNESS AT A DISTANT ESTATE KNOWN AS THORNFIELD...

MRS. FAIRFAX, I BELIEVE?

YOU ARE JANE EYRE! HOW DO YOU DO, MY DEAR? I'M AFRAID YOU HAD A TEDIOUS RIDE. YOU MUST BE COLD — COME TO THE FIRE.

SHE TREATS ME AS A VISITOR! I NEVER ANTICIPATED SUCH A WARM RECEPTION BUT I MUST NOT EXULT TOO SOON!

SHALL I HAVE THE PLEASURE OF SEEING MISS FAIRFAX, MY PUPIL, TONIGHT?

MISS FAIRFAX? OH, YOU MEAN MISS VARENS. VARENS IS THE NAME OF YOUR FUTURE PUPIL.

INDEED! THEN SHE IS NOT YOUR DAUGHTER?

NO, I HAVE NO FAMILY BUT I'LL NOT KEEP YOU SITTING UP LATE TONIGHT — YOU MUST BE TIRED! I'LL SHOW YOU YOUR BEDROOM.

NEXT MORNING...

WHAT! OUT ALREADY? I SEE YOU ARE AN EARLY RISER.

MRS. FAIRFAX RECEIVED HER WITH AN AFFABLE KISS AND SHAKE OF THE HAND...

C'EST LAS MA GOUVERNANTE? *

MAIS OUI, * CERTAINMENT!

*IS THAT MY GOVERNESS?

* WHY OF COURSE!

THEY SPEAK FRENCH! ARE THEY FOREIGNERS?

ADELE WAS BORN ON THE CONTINENT! MR. ROCHESTER BROUGHT HER HERE JUST RECENTLY! I DARESAY YOU WILL NOT HAVE ANY TROUBLE CONVERSING WITH HER IN HER NATIVE TONGUE!

IT DID NOT TAKE JANE LONG TO MAKE FRIENDS WITH HER LITTLE CHARGE, CONVERSING WITH HER IN FRENCH!

AND I CAN SING OPERA JUST LIKE MY MAMA USED TO DO! DO YOU WANT TO HEAR ME SING, NOW?

WELL, YOU CERTAINLY ARE A GIRL OF MANY TALENTS, ADELE! I SHALL DO SO DIRECTLY AFTER BREAKFAST!

THAT AFTERNOON, MRS. FAIRFAX TOOK JANE TO THE ROOF OF THE HOUSE TO SHOW HER THE VIEW OF THE COUNTRYSIDE, AS THEY DESCENDED FROM THE ATTIC...

SUDDENLY, A LOUD, HIDEOUS LAUGH CAME FROM ONE OF THE ROOMS...

WHAT WAS THAT?

Ha..Ha.. Haaa..

IN THE MONTHS THAT FOLLOWED JANE HEARD THAT PIERCING LAUGH FREQUENTLY. SOMEHOW SHE COULD NOT CONNECT THAT WEIRD SOUND WITH GRACE POOLE, WHO WENT ABOUT HER WORK CALMLY AND QUIETLY, ALTHOUGH THERE WAS AN AIR OF MYSTERY ABOUT HER JANE COULD NOT QUITE FATHOM...

ONE AFTERNOON IN JANUARY, JANE VOLUNTEERED TO POST A LETTER FOR MRS. FAIRFAX IN NEARBY HAY...

SUDDENLY...

OH, WHAT A FINE LOOKING ANIMAL!

A HORSEMAN FOLLOWED IN THE WAKE OF THE ANIMAL...

A MOMENT LATER...

THE HORSE MUST HAVE SLIPPED ON THE ICY PAVEMENT! I'LL SEE IF HE NEEDS ANY HELP!

AS SHE APPROACHED THE RIDER WAVED HER AWAY...

I CANNOT THINK OF LEAVING YOU, SIR, IN THIS SOLITARY LANE, TILL I SEE YOU ARE FIT TO MOUNT YOUR HORSE!

YOU HAVE GUESSED IT! I AM GLAD YOU ARE THE ONLY PERSON BESIDES MYSELF WHO KNOWS WHAT HAS HAPPENED! I SHALL RETIRE TO THE SOFA IN THE LIBRARY FOR THE REST OF THE NIGHT!

GOOD NIGHT, THEN SIR!

WHAT! ARE YOU LEAVING ALREADY? WHY, YOU HAVE SAVED MY LIFE! SNATCHED ME FROM A HORRIBLE DEATH! AT LEAST, SHAKE HANDS!

I HAVE A PLEASURE IN OWING YOU SO GREAT A DEBT! I CANNOT SAY MORE!

GOOD-NIGHT AGAIN, SIR! THERE IS NO DEBT OR OBLIGATION IN THE CASE!

I KNEW YOU WOULD DO ME GOOD IN SOME WAY- I SAW IT IN YOUR EYES WHEN I FIRST BEHELD YOU! MY CHERISHED PRESERVER, GOOD-NIGHT!

STRANGE ENERGY WAS IN HIS VOICE - STRANGE FIRE IN HIS LOOK...

AGAIN, SHE MADE AN ATTEMPT TO LEAVE HIM...

BUT YOU MUST NOT GO YET, JANE!

I AM COLD, SIR - AND I THINK I HEAR MRS. FAIRFAX IN THE HALL!

HE RELAXED HIS FINGERS AND SHE WAS GONE...

A FEW WEEKS LATER, WHILE MR. ROCHESTER WAS ENTERTAINING SOME FRIENDS IN THE DRAWING ROOM...

WON'T YOU SING FOR US, MR. ROCHESTER?

COMMANDS FROM MISS INGRAM'S LIPS WOULD BREATHE SPIRIT INTO A MUG OF MILK AND WATER!

JANE HAD CLOSELY OBSERVED MR. ROCHESTER'S ATTENTION TO MISS INGRAM EVER SINCE THE ARRIVAL OF THE GUESTS...

I THINK THIS IS A GOOD TIME FOR ME TO SLIP AWAY!

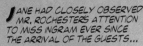

AND A LITTLE DEPRESSED! WHAT ABOUT? TELL ME!

NOTHING, NOTHING, SIR!

A HALF HOUR LATER

SO THERE YOU ARE! RETURN TO THE DRAWING ROOM; YOU ARE DESERTING TOO EARLY!

I AM TIRED SIR!

WHY, I CAN SEE THE TEARS GATHERING IN YOUR EYES! ALL RIGHT, I'LL EXCUSE YOU TONIGHT! BUT UNDERSTAND, IT IS MY WISH THAT YOU APPEAR IN THE DRAWING ROOM, GUESTS OR NO GUESTS!

NOW, GO AND SEND SOPHIE FOR ADELE! GOODNIGHT, MY...

HE STOPPED, BIT HIS LIPS, AND ABRUPTLY LEFT...

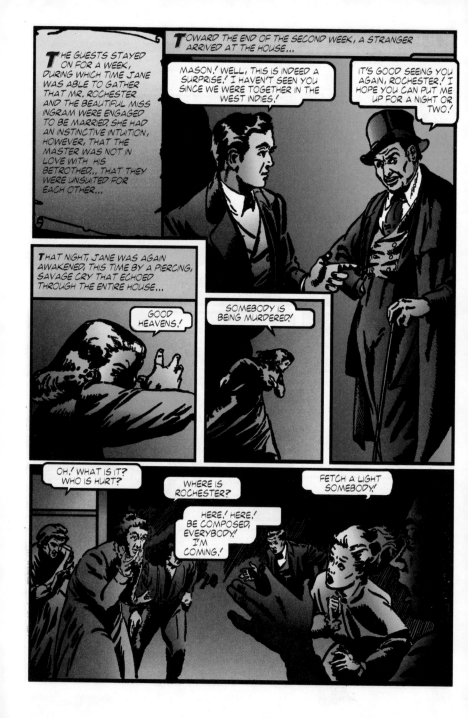

THE WEDDING WAS SET FOR A MONTH LATER, DURING WHICH TIME THEY MADE FREQUENT TRIPS TO MILLCOTE TOGETHER, TO BUY JANE'S BRIDAL OUTFIT. FINALLY, THE FATAL DAY ARRIVED. IT WAS TO BE AN INFORMAL CEREMONY AT THE OLD THORNFIELD CHURCH...

THE TWO FIGURES FOUND A REMOTE CORNER AS THE COUPLE ENTERED...

AS THEY APPROACHED THE CHURCH, JANE SAW TWO MEN SLINKING IN AT THE OPEN DOOR...

I'M SURE I'VE SEEN ONE OF THOSE MEN BEFORE! HE LOOKS STRANGELY FAMILIAR!

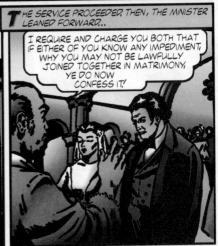

THE SERVICE PROCEEDED. THEN, THE MINISTER LEANED FORWARD...

I REQUIRE AND CHARGE YOU BOTH THAT IF EITHER OF YOU KNOW ANY IMPEDIMENT, WHY YOU MAY NOT BE LAWFULLY JOINED TOGETHER IN MATRIMONY, YE DO NOW CONFESS IT!

SUDDENLY, A VOICE, CLOSE AT HAND, SPOKE UP...

THE MARRIAGE CANNOT GO ON! I DECLARE THE EXISTENCE OF AN IMPEDIMENT!

MR. MASON!

JANE BREATHED A SIGH OF RELIEF. SHE HAD DREADED WORSE – HAD EXPECTED TO HEAR THAT EDWARD WAS HOPELESSLY MAD...

THE INNKEEPER WENT ON...

HE WOULDN'T LEAVE THE HOUSE TILL EVERY ONE ELSE WAS OUT OF THE HOUSE BEFORE HIM, THE ROOF CRASHED AND HIS HAND WAS BADLY HURT – HAD TO BE AMPUTATED!

WHERE IS HE? WHERE DOES HE LIVE, NOW?

AT FERDEAN, ON A FARM HE HAS, ABOUT THIRTY MILES OFF, QUITE A DESOLATE SPOT. HE'D HAVE NONE BUT OLD JOHN AND HIS WIFE WITH HIM!

POOR, POOR EDWARD! VICTIM OF CRUEL FATE AND A MADWOMAN TO WHOM HIS SENSE OF LOYALTY BOUND HIM TO THE VERY END! I'LL GO TO HIM AT ONCE!

SHE ARRIVED AT FERDEAN JUST BEFORE DARK...

JANE EYRE
CHARLOTTE BRONTE

In the best adventure stories, the hero triumphs over a difficult beginning, often unloved and unaided, and finds happiness in the end. If you accept that growing up is an adventure for each one of us, you can understand why Charlotte Brontë's *Jane Eyre* is one of the most widely read and admired novels ever written. The book describes—with painstaking detail and passion—the "adventure" of its heroine as she grows into a strong, honorable and passionate woman. And it does so with all the fixin's of melodrama: lost heirs, madwomen in the attic, foreign brides and gypsy fortunetellers!

Jane Eyre was highly praised when it was published in 1847, and was popular enough with the public to go through three editions by the following year—terrific for a first novel by an unknown author. Although the book has been read and re-read for almost 150 years, there have been a series of pretty radical shifts in how it has been viewed: critics have treated *Jane Eyre* as everything from a template for Harlequin romances to a radical feminist tract to an apology for colonial imperialism. But when it was published, not everyone found the book so appealing: some early reviewers were troubled by Jane's failure to act in socially acceptable ways, and by the book's critical attitude toward conventional religion, the upper classes, and Victorian notions of the appropriate behavior of women.

The Author

The Brontë family is rather better known than most literary families, in part because of its dramatic and tragic history. Although many of the elements of *Jane Eyre* are traceable to Charlotte's life, it seems extraordinary that a woman with her background could have written such a novel. Brontë's father was born in Ireland to a poor family; he rose above his beginnings to attend Cambridge University, became a priest in the Church of England, and changed his name from Prunty to the more refined Brontë. By doing so, he raised himself, and his family, into the middle class, though they were always very poor. He married Maria Branwell and they had six children in quick succession: Maria, Elizabeth, Charlotte (1816), Patrick (called Branwell), Emily, and Anne. Sadly, Mrs. Brontë died of cancer when Charlotte was five; the children were raised by their father and their aunt, who came to live with the family after their mother's death.

Like *Jane Eyre*, Charlotte Brontë and her two older sisters, Maria and Elizabeth, went to a charity boarding school when they were quite young. Like the Lowood Institution in *Jane Eyre*, Charlotte's school was strict, unhealthy, and poorly run. Maria (who was apparently the model for Helen Burns in Jane Eyre) and Elizabeth fell ill and died when Charlotte was nine.

Her father removed Charlotte from the school and brought her home to Haworth, a tiny, isolated village on the Yorkshire moors.

During the next several years the children were educated at home, reading literature, newspapers, and magazines. She and her brother and sisters depended upon each other for stimulation and amusement. The children were very close, inventing imaginary worlds full of the romance and excitement that were missing from their lives. Their poetry and plays were full of supernatural characters, fantastic plots, and faraway kingdoms. Many of these romantic elements appear in altered forms in the novels of Anne, Emily, and Charlotte.

Over the next ten years Charlotte left home for brief periods several times. She was sent to another, more pleasant, boarding school, to which she later returned as a teacher; twice she took governess jobs. These lonely, sometimes unpleasant experiences showed Charlotte that she didn't want to live away from her home and siblings. She and her sisters decided to set up a school at the parsonage. To prepare, Charlotte and Emily went to school in Brussels to learn French and German. There she developed a strong attachment to the husband of the director of the school, M. Heger. It's tempting to see this as Charlotte's grand passion, but there's really very little evidence about their relationship. In any case, Heger apparently did not return her sentiments, and after Charlotte returned to Haworth he did not answer her letters.

When their school project failed (no students applied), and Charlotte's beloved brother Branwell returned home in drunken disgrace, Charlotte, Emily, and Anne tried their hands at authorship, publishing a book of poems in 1846. It sold exactly two copies. The sisters persisted: each wrote a novel, and they attempted to publish them together as a three-volume work. But only Emily's *Wuthering Heights* and Anne's *Agnes Grey* found a publisher. Charlotte's *The Professor* was rejected many times and was not published during her lifetime. She wrote *Jane Eyre* while *The Professor* was making the rounds of publishers, and it was published to widespread praise in 1847. Charlotte's triumph didn't last very long. In 1848, as she was working on a new novel, her brother died; Emily died the same year. Anne's health also declined rapidly, and she died the following year, leaving Charlotte, at 33, the only surviving child. She published two more novels, *Shirley* (1849) and *Villette* (1853), neither of which received much favorable comment at the time.

During this sad and lonely period, Charlotte received her third proposal of marriage and, this time, said "yes." Sadly, marriage did not mark the beginning of a happy and fulfilled life as it does for Jane Eyre. Charlotte became pregnant and, suffering from complications of the pregnancy, died in 1855 at the age of 39.

Characters

The cast of characters in Jane Eyre is fairly small, and only a handful are really important. At the beginning of the novel, we meet Mrs. Reed, a rich, snobbish, cold woman who dotes on her own children and finds it impossible to love Jane. John Reed is a spoiled bully who treats Jane with cruelty and contempt. The daughters are at opposite extremes. Eliza is a sour, miserly child, and Georgiana is a pretty, vain, foolish girl who is pampered and spoiled. Mr. Brocklehurst, the stern and forbidding director of Lowood, is a cruel, hypocritical man who believes in self-denial, hunger, cold, and strict discipline for the lower-class girls in his school, and status, privilege, and comfort for himself and the upper-classes.

PRESENTLY JANE ENTERED THE ROOM....

HERE COMES THAT LITTLE BRAT!

SHE HAS A NERVE, COMING IN HERE! WHO DOES SHE THINK SHE IS?

Once Jane is sent off to Lowood, she comes into contact with Miss Temple, the school superintendent, who provides a model for Jane of an independent, intelligent, refined, kind, accomplished, and spirited woman (she even stands up to Mr. Brocklehurst on occasion). Through her influence, Jane learns to control her emotions and becomes a well-educated and disciplined young woman. Helen Burns provides a different kind of model, one of saintly patience. Jane can admire her certainty of a paradise after death, and the way she calmly bears punishment, hardship, and ridicule, but Jane cares too much for people and relationships to try to imitate her.

Edward Fairfax Rochester, the wealthy Master of Thornfield, is a complex figure. He is moody, quick-tempered, and restless. He's had a series of European mistresses. He is, as Jane says, "an ugly man," but intelligent, perceptive, physically powerful, and of equally strong character. He is a fine horseman, an accomplished musician and actor, and an astute businessman. And he is a passionate lover who has searched for years for a woman worthy of his love. After he is maimed and blinded and his lunatic wife dies, Rochester is morally and spiritually rehabilitated; under Jane's influence he becomes a loving husband, companion, and friend.

Blanche Ingram, Jane's rival for Rochester's love, is beautiful, well-educated, and aristocratic. But she is also arrogant, heartless, shallow, and spoiled, and has, as Jane says, "a poor mind." She seems chiefly interested in Rochester's money.

Bertha Mason, Rochester's mad wife, can hardly be said to be a character. Instead, she's a brooding presence at Thornfield, threatening Rochester's peace of mind and even his life, haunting Thornfield with her maniacal laugh-

Plain Jane?

As you read the novel, you can see that the illustrations of the Classics Illustrated adaptation are not uniformly faithful to the book. The Reeds and Brocklehurst fit their portraits in the novel quite well, as does Miss Temple. However, the CI adaptation tends to glamorize both Rochester and Jane. In the novel, Brontë makes much of Rochester's square forehead, blocky

ter, stalking Jane before the wedding (and symbolically tearing the veil in half) and, through her brother's intervention, separating Jane from Rochester.

Hardly seen in the CI adaptation, Mary and Diana Rivers, like Miss Temple, are role models for Jane; they are intelligent, kind, and accomplished. When the Rivers family takes Jane in, they provide her with the familial love and companionship she has missed all her life, even before we discover that they are her cousins.

St. John Rivers, Rochester's rival for Jane's love, is described as handsome as a Greek god. A devout and tireless parish priest and eloquent orator, he plans to become a missionary in India. Like Helen Burns, his thoughts are fixed on Heaven rather than earth. He rejects the love of the beautiful daughter of a wealthy local land-owner, although he loves her too, or even because he loves her. He has the potential to be a great man, but Jane rightly concludes that he is too rigid, self-denying, and ambitious to be a good husband.

Jane Eyre's character is central to the meaning of the novel, and she grows and changes with her experiences, while retaining the independence, passion, and inner strength that make readers fall in love with her from the first page. At the beginning of the novel we see a lonely child who wants to be loved and accepted, but is excluded, snubbed, and bullied. Her emotional outbursts at John and Mrs. Reed show a surprising moral power for a ten-year-old. Her progress at Lowood shows her learning to control her emotions and excelling in her studies despite the hardships of the school. It is important that she also wants something more than Lowood, some wider, more satisfying life. The fact that Jane herself moves to find herself a position as governess shows further strength and independence.

Jane's life at Thornfield shows another kind of growth and flowering, for here she meets Rochester and comes to love him. Even in their first conversations, her directness, honesty, and self-possession surprise, charm, and attract him. When Rochester, with apparent cruelty, makes her believe he will marry Blanche Ingram and send Jane off to work in Ireland, Jane shows her true power in a wonderful scene in which she explodes at him and declares herself his equal.

When the delirious happiness that follows Rochester's proposal is destroyed at the church and the wedding is called off, Jane finds even greater strength and refuses to be his mistress. She leaves Thornfield. The suffering she endures before she is taken in by the Rivers family strengthens her for the even greater struggle it takes to resist St. John's insistence that she marry him and join in a noble religious cause that she knows will kill her. Jane's happy ending is a just reward for her strength of character and her unwillingness to compromise principle or emotion.

build—his ugliness (by Victorian standards). As for Jane, Brontë portrays her as small and plain—it's important to the meaning of the book that Jane is, as she says, "poor, obscure, plain, and little" and can't get by on her looks.

Plot

The plot of *Jane Eyre* is fairly simple to describe. Jane Eyre is an orphan taken in by her uncle's family, the Reeds, and raised by her aunt after the uncle dies. The aunt does not like the child and sends her off to a boarding school for poor children. She rises to the head of her class and becomes a teacher, but then decides to broaden her horizons by becoming a governess.

She accepts a position in a large country house as governess of a single young child, the ward of Mr. Rochester, the absent master of the house. When Rochester returns, he seeks out and questions her and he comes to respect and like her. They fall in love. He pretends to court an aristocratic young woman, goading Jane into speaking her love. He proposes, and they plan a wedding. The ceremony is broken off when they learn that Rochester is already married, and that his mad wife has been

living in the attic of the house for years. The secret is revealed by the woman's brother and his lawyer, who arrive just in time from Jamaica. Rochester asks Jane to run away to Europe, but she refuses and runs away.

Penniless and starving, Jane finds herself at the door of St. John Rivers and his two sisters, Mary and Diana. Jane lives under a false name, and takes a job as the teacher of a village school. When her true identity is accidentally revealed, the Riverses discover that she is really their long lost cousin and the heir to their uncle's wine fortune. (The uncle's lawyer turns out to be the same one who helped to disrupt Jane's wedding; the tale he tells St. John of the disappearing governess arouses St. John's suspicions.) Jane insists on sharing her inheritance with her new-found cousins, and they begin a happy time of reading, discussion, learning, and companionship.

St. John, however, is preparing for his ambitious plan to become a missionary in India. He persuades Jane to help him learn Hindustani, and later asks her to marry him and come to India to help him in his work. She resists: she doesn't love him and knows he does not love her. Still, his religious zeal and the worthiness of his cause sways her. She is on the verge of agreeing to marry him when she hears Rochester's disembodied voice calling her name and leaves to find out what has happened to him. When she returns to Thornfield, Rochester is gone, the house is in ruins, and his mad wife is dead. She finds him living in seclusion, blind and maimed. Jane marries him and nurses him back to health, and he regains his sight in time to see his first-born son. Here the story ends in happiness, wealth, and true love.

Stated baldly the plot is preposterous. The mad woman hidden in the attic for years, the incredible coincidence of Jane ending up homeless on the doorstep of cousins she didn't know she had, the inheritance that makes Jane independent, the amazing coincidence that Bertha Rochester's family know Jane's uncle and use the same lawyer, and finally Rochester's supernaturally amplified voice ringing across the moors, saving Jane from an early death in India-- together these should push the novel into melodramatic absurdity. But for most readers they don't: each separate absurdity is present for a purpose other than simple sensationalism. Jane herself sweeps most readers irresistibly along.

One reason for this is that long sections of the novel are both reasonable and logical. Charlotte Brontë draws the early scenes clearly and convincingly, especially Jane's sense of unjust accusation. Her unusual vehemence and power strike most readers as believable. This is partly because the story is told by the mature, happy Jane, whose recollections of her childhood and her childish feelings are insightful and characteristically honest. The wonderful portrait of young Jane at Lowood—her difficulties and progress toward maturity and self-control—feel natural and in keeping with her character. Her restlessness after Miss Temple leaves also seems psychologically right: once Miss Temple's guiding presence is removed, Jane longs for liberty, or, if that seems too grand, "at least a new servitude."

The move to Thornfield, too, is brilliantly handled. Jane's pleasure in her new situation, the beauty of the country and the house, her success with Adele, and Mrs. Fairfax's approval all temporarily calm her restlessness.

Jane's calm is disrupted forever when the brooding, fiery Rochester charges in on his big black horse with his huge dog running along beside and begins a process that will test her to the utmost.

The interviews by the fire which Charlotte Brontë uses to show the progress of Jane and Rochester's feelings for each other are handled with a kind of magical charm that makes their growing love, seem to grow naturally from the compatibility of their spirits despite their differences in age, experience, and class. The small, poor, plain governess turns out to be original, forthright, independent, and spirited, and the stern and quick-tempered Rochester turns out to be a very keen judge of character who can charm and amuse as well as brood.

The visit of the Ingrams and their upper-class friends is perhaps less successfully handled, but it succeeds in its main purpose of clarifying the characters of Rochester and Jane, as does the fantastic episode in which Rochester comes in dressed as a gypsy and insists on telling the fortunes of all the unmarried women. In fact, it is Rochester who gives one of the most telling portraits of Jane as he (disguised as a gypsy woman) pretends to read her fortune in her face. He tells her that everything seems favorable (we can see, as Jane can't, that he means favorable for their marriage) except for the forehead, which tells him:

> "I can live alone, if self-respect and circumstances require me so to do. I need not sell my soul to buy bliss. I have an inward treasure born with me, which can keep me alive if all extraneous delights should be withheld, or offered only at a price I cannot afford to give."

But just when Rochester seems on the brink of revealing his love, Jane receives a message summoning her to see her aunt Reed. That visit prolongs our suspense, and conveniently allows Mrs. Reed to reveal the existence of Jane's

uncle, setting up the possibility of a future inheritance. What's more important, it shows the change her years away have made in Jane: she takes control of the household, listens calmly when her aunt tells her that she deliberately kept Jane's uncle from finding her, and forgives the dying woman. This self-control would have been impossible for the younger Jane, and it prepares us for Jane's actions when her marriage is broken off.

When Jane returns to Thornfield and what she believes will be a brief stay until Rochester's marriage to Blanche Ingram, Brontë wisely does not make us wait too long for the wonderful scene in which Rochester asks her to marry him. We get no conventionally romantic proposal scene with him on bended knee. Instead it's a painful scene: he goads Jane into declaring her love, first by pretending he will marry Blanche. Her response, with its ringing declaration of their equality, is perhaps the most powerful and moving passage in the novel, and it puts Jane in a category by herself in fiction up to Brontë's time:

Do you think I can stay to become nothing to you? Do you think I am an automaton?—a machine without feelings? and can bear to have my morsel of bread snatched from my lips, and my drop of living water dashed from my cup? Do you think, because I am poor, obscure, plain, and little, I am soulless and heartless? You think wrong!—I have as much soul as you—and full as much heart! And if God had gifted me with some beauty and much wealth, I should have made it as hard for you to leave me, as it is now for me to leave you. I am not talking to you now through the medium of custom, conventionalities, nor even of mortal flesh: it is my spirit that addresses your spirit; just as if both had passed through the grave, and we stood at God's feet, equal -- as we are!

This is what Rochester has been longing for: a woman of independence, fire, and individuality. But happiness does not come so easily for Jane. At the church, Bertha's brother appears, the secret of the mad wife is revealed, and the wedding is broken off.

Rochester asks Jane to defy convention and come with him to Europe to live with him as his mistress. Jane refuses. The life he describes might seem like paradise, but living as his mistress would violate Jane's principles. Modern readers have difficulty understanding Jane's decision, but it allows Brontë to show us just how strong Jane's sense of herself is. And it is easy to see that Jane is now in control even of her passions, strong as they are.

Jane decides that she must leave Thornfield, and sneaks away in the early morning, purchasing a ticket on a pass-

Why Do They *Do* That?

To understand why Jane, Rochester, and others in the book behave as they do, it's helpful to recall a few things about Victorian society:

- **Why doesn't Rochester divorce Bertha and marry Jane?**
  At the time Jane Eyre was written, divorce in England was impossible except by Act of Parliament; and it was impossible (and dishonorable as well) to divorce a spouse who was mad.

- **Why doesn't Jane just go live in Europe with Rochester?**
  Not only would Jane violate her

ing coach. This leaves her penniless, on a remote moor where she is forced to beg for food and sleep in the heather. Exhausted, suffering from hunger and exposure, she finds herself at a small house. Inside she sees two young women talking by the fire. She knocks, asking for shelter, is initially turned away by a servant, but is taken in by the man of the house returning late from his duties as parish priest.

Jane recovers physically and emotionally with the Rivers family, asking only shelter and help in finding some employment, and keeping her name and story a mystery. She enjoys learning and reading with them and finds herself elevated and cheered by their friendship and high regard. St. John eventually gets her a post as the village school teacher, and she finds herself independent and relatively content. This part of the novel shows us that Jane has indeed matured, and that Rochester's assessment of her character was right: she can live alone if she has to.

St. John and his sisters receive news that their uncle has died, but without leaving them any of his fortune because of an old quarrel he had with their father. Instead, he has left his money to another niece, his only other relative.

St. John accidentally discovers Jane's true identity and explains to her that she is now wealthy. When Jane discovers how large the fortune is and that she is their cousin, she insists on sharing it with them. In the happy times that follow, St. John, who is preparing for his life's work as a missionary in India, persuades Jane to help him learn Hindustani. Their relationship, and her admiration for his integrity, give him a kind of power over her: it's difficult for Jane when he asks her to marry him and come to India. But Jane has known real love. She does not love him and sees that he does not love her. When she offers to go as his helper, not as his wife, St. John insists, using all of his religious power to convince her that she must come. Although she has been unable to find out what has happened to Rochester, she begins to feel that she cannot resist St. John. She asks for God's guidance, and, as she prays, feels a kind of jolt and hears Rochester's voice calling her name.

Jane travels to Thornfield, but finds it a ruin. She learns that Rochester's mad wife caused the fire in which she was killed despite Rochester's attempt to save her: Rochester himself was maimed and blinded. Learning this, Jane goes to him. The two lovers are reunited, and, after a short time they are married, Rochester regains his sight, and they live in perfect happiness, as equal partners and best friends.

religious principles by "living in sin" with Rochester; doing so would mean no decent family would employ her as a governess, servant, teacher... If Jane and Rochester broke up, she would have no economic alternative but to be someone else's mistress--or to die.

- **Okay, then why does St. John insist Jane marry him?**
  (See answer above!) The Victorians believed strongly that it was not proper for a man and woman, unmarried and not closely related, to travel, live, or even work together without chaperones.

In some ways, theme is of secondary importance in Jane Eyre. This is Jane's autobiography, and, as such, it needs no other theme. But the autobiography is a fiction, however much readers are caught up in Jane's difficult but triumphant life. It is possible to trace some very significant ideas throughout the book.

Women in Society

Jane Eyre attacks conventional ideas about the place and nature of women, and asserts the intellectual and moral equality of men and women in a way that many of Brontë's contemporaries found disturbing. Victorian society had very restricted ideas about what women were fit to do and about how they should behave. Few

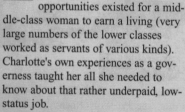

opportunities existed for a middle-class woman to earn a living (very large numbers of the lower classes worked as servants of various kinds). Charlotte's own experiences as a governess taught her all she needed to know about that rather underpaid, low-status job.

Brontë's women characters demonstrate just how important independence and usefulness are to her. Miss Temple shows Jane that a cultured, well-educated woman can hold a responsible, valuable position, earn her own living, and retain her self-respect (though she eventually marries off Miss Temple to a clergyman). Mrs. Fairfax, too, has a responsible job that gives her independence. And Jane's own positions as teacher and governess allow her to retain her middle-class status and earn her own (small) income.

In some ways the plight of Diana and Mary Rivers mirrors Charlotte's own situation. They have very little money, and their marriage prospects are grim. They become governesses because that is nearly the only socially acceptable position they can hold. Jane's fortune eventually provides financial independence for them, and that leads naturally to happy marriages as well—wealth frees a woman to marry for love rather than money. As for Jane, she becomes useful and independent as the village school teacher. The difficulty for Jane (and Charlotte) is that none of these jobs are really adequate. They have no

status, the income is very low, and they do not provide enough scope for intelligent and able women.

The upper class women had even fewer choices. While John Reed is sent off to college to become a lawyer, his two sisters are trapped by their class and gender. Georgiana, beautiful and silly, goes out into society and eventually marries a "wealthy, worn-out man of fashion;" the marriage ends her existence rather than beginning it. Her sister Eliza takes another time-honored route, becoming the Superior of a convent. Although this position is a responsible, independent, and useful one, the sacrifice it requires is too great for Jane. In the same way, the Ingrams are idle creatures preoccupied with parties, money, marriage, and class. They are cultured but do nothing useful. Rosamund Oliver is a more positive example of what a wealthy young woman could expect. While she waits for a marriage proposal, she helps at the village school; there is no thought of her working. Here is a rare place where Brontë seems blinded by the financial independence of upper class women: she can't see just how restricted their paths were.

As strong as Brontë's challenge to conventional ideas is, Jane Eyre is no feminist tract, as Jane's own story shows us. The large inheritance from her uncle frees her from her job as school teacher, but it also "frees" her from useful work altogether. (To be fair, is there anyone who hasn't daydreamed about what they would do if they were suddenly rich and could quit working?) She follows the conventional path to marriage and motherhood and apparently contents herself with running her household, raising her children, overseeing the education of Adele, and exchanging visits with Diana and Mary.

Social Class

Class and social standing are still important in our society, but they were much more important in Victorian England, and much less changeable. Perhaps because of her own family's rise from poverty to the middle class and her employment as a governess for upper-class families, Charlotte Brontë, through Jane, has difficulty seeing the lower classes as anything but coarse and ignorant, and the upper class as anything but arrogant and self-absorbed. Early in the novel, the doctor who comes to see her after her terror in the red room asks if she would like to go to live with her poor relatives. In spite of her cruel treatment at Gateshead, she rejects the idea.

I could not see how poor people had the means of being kind; and then to learn to speak like them, to adopt their manners, to be uneducated, to grow up like one of the poor women I saw sometimes nursing their children or washing their clothes at the cottage doors of the village of Gateshead: no, I was not heroic enough to purchase liberty at the price of caste.

It is clear even at the end of the novel that Jane has difficulty putting aside her prejudice. When faced with her twenty scholars at the village school at Morton, she finds that only a few of them can read, all speak in a local dialect, and many are coarse and ignorant. Although she tries to remind herself that their flesh and blood is as good as any one from the gentry, she says,

I felt -- yes, idiot that I am -- I felt degraded....I was weakly dismayed at the ignorance, the poverty, the coarseness of all I heard and saw round me.

If she finds the lower classes inferior, she shows outright hostility toward the aristocracy. We have already seen her harsh portrait of Blanche Ingram; the two titled Ladies don't fare very well either. Jane finds them haughty-looking, fierce, hard, "furrowed with pride," and finds Lady Ingram's voice intolerably dogmatic. Young Lord Ingram seems to her "apathetic and listless." They do not endear themselves to Jane (or the reader) by gossiping about former governesses as if Jane weren't there.

This notion of class and social status is reflected in the nature of the happy ending of the novel as well. This is not Cinderella, and Rochester is no prince. Rather, once Jane gets her inheritance, they are both independent, middle-class, respectable. Rochester's maiming and blinding even makes them more nearly equal physically, by requiring him to depend on her. The resulting picture of perfect marriage is of course not restricted to the middle class, but in Brontë's mind it may have been.

Religion

Religion plays a large role in the novel as well. On this subject, too, Charlotte Brontë was much criticized. None of her religious characters is completely admirable. Brocklehurst, of course, is a cruel, hypocritical enforcer of social privilege. The goal of his school is to produce plain, humble, docile girls who will be useful tools for wealthier people. The means to his ends are hell-fire religion, deprivation, and hardship. His own wife and daughters, in contrast, live in the comfort to which their class entitles them.

Catholicism, in the person of Eliza Reed, doesn't fare much better. As Eliza describes it, Catholicism is a rigid, restrictive, and unnatural system; and Jane considers life as a nun to be like being "walled up alive in a French convent."

Helen Burns and St. John Rivers, sincere and mostly positive figures, show Brontë's distrust of religion that places too much emphasis on the next life. Helen's passivity, resignation, and faith in Heaven have Jane's admiration, but she finds these ideas life-denying and almost inhuman. St. John's great cause is admirable in itself, but his personal ambition and his stern devotion to that cause make him such a cold, insensitive man.

Jane's own feelings about religion are never very distinctly explained, except as distinguished from St. John's. Although Brontë marries off Miss Temple and Mary Rivers to clergymen, we learn nothing about the men except that they are worthy of their brides. Rochester's religion is similarly vague. Although he is ready to violate the Church's ideas about the sanctity of marriage, he recovers his faith after his injuries.

Love

The importance and value of romantic love is perhaps the most obvious of Brontë's themes. Remarkable as the passionate young Jane is, she does not reach her full potential until she falls in love with Rochester. In true romantic fashion, their love improves both of them: Rochester becomes kinder, happier, more gentle; plain Jane even becomes prettier.

This is no Ken and Barbie love, based on doe-eyed glances and longing sighs. Jane's plainness and Rochester's ugliness, and the barriers of age, class, and experience, elevate this love story to a different level. By implication at least,

HE STOOD IN MUTE DEVOTION...

Brontë places the importance of romantic love on at least an equal plane with religious devotion, as she shows by having Jane reject St. John's noble religious cause to return to Rochester.

As important as romantic love is in Jane Eyre, it is not what makes this novel endure. What makes the story so memorable is Charlotte Brontë's portrait of Jane, who goes from unloved and unwanted orphan to mature, independent, secure woman, the loving partner of a loving, sympathetic, and thoroughly compatible husband. It is Brontë's sympathy for Jane, and her ability to portray the secrets of an extraordinary human soul, that make this book a classic.

• *Jane Eyre* is full of doubles or contrasting pairs: Bertha can be seen as a double for Jane, a kind of warning about what uncontrolled passions can lead to. Rochester/St. John, Blanche/Rosamund, Eliza and Georgiana/Diana and Mary are other possible pairs or doubles. How do such doubles work? What do they do for the novel?

• What does Jane really think about religion? Consider the evidence: her reactions to  Brocklehurst, Helen Burns, Eliza Reed, Rochester, and St. John, combined with her actions (especially church attendance, prayer, and her rejection of Rochester's proposal).

• Rochester's maiming and blinding can be seen as punishment for his attempted bigamy. Do they also provide a lesson for him about dependency? Force him to depend on Jane at the end? Are male power and dominance one of Brontë's targets? Why can't he remain the powerful, fiery figure he is at the beginning?

• Setting and weather are significant in Jane Eyre. consider the raw winter day at the beginning of the novel, or the Midsummer-eve on which Rochester proposes, followed by the lightning storm that symbolically splits a huge tree as their newly pledged union is to be split? Can you think of other weather images from the book?

• There are many supernatural elements in Jane Eyre; the ghost in the red room, Jane's dream of Thornfield in ruins, her vision of a white human form speaking through clouds and telling her to leave Thornfield after the wedding is broken up, and of course Rochester's voice across the moors keeping her from marrying St. John. Do these elements distract you from the story? Do they make you expect a different kind of story than you get?

• Describe Jane Eyre's (or Charlotte Brontë's) views of marriage, using as evidence all the marriages that are described even briefly in the novel. (There are at least ten marriages to consider.)

• Why is the end the end? Some readers have been unhappy with the happy ending of the novel. Can you imagine a "better" ending?

CREDITS

David Hoover holds a PhD from Indiana University, and is an Associate Professor in the English Department at New York University.

Jane Eyre

art by Harley M. Griffiths

Classics Illustrated: Jane Eyre © Twin Circle Publishing Co.,
a division of Frawley Enterprises; licensed to First Classics, Inc.
All new material and compilation © 1996 by Acclaim Books, Inc.

Dale-Chall R.L.: 7.2

ISBN 1-57840-005-8

Classics Illustrated® is a registered trademark
of the Frawley Corporation.

Acclaim Books, New York, NY
Printed in the United States

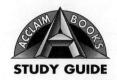

STUDY GUIDE